Judaica
PRESS

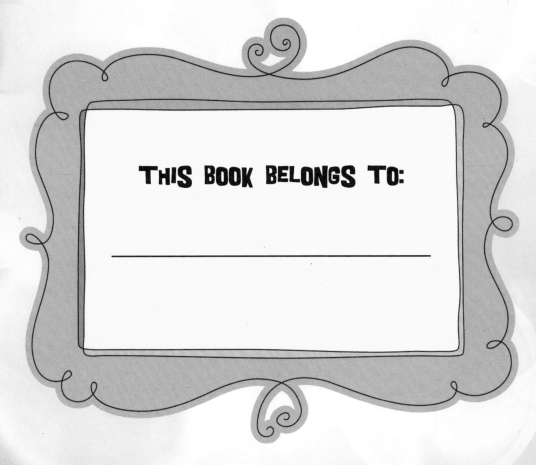

THIS BOOK BELONGS TO:

_____

I Can Be
מַכִּיר טוֹב

BY SARA BLAU
ILLUSTRATED BY MALKA WOLF

Judaica
PRESS

THE JUDAICA PRESS, INC.
123 Ditmas Avenue / Brooklyn, NY 11218
718-972-6200 / 800-972-6201
info@judaicapress.com
www.judaicapress.com

A NOTE TO PARENTS

Dear Parents,

We all want our kids to acquire the wonderful middah of hakaras hatov (gratitude). As the Chovos Halevavos teaches in Shaar Habechinah, hakaras hatov is the foundation of all avodas Hashem. The more we think about and appreciate all the benefits we receive from Hashem and His many shlichim (our parents, friends, teachers, etc.), the more we recognize our obligation to follow His will. But hakaras hatov also has the effect of making us happier people, by helping us realize how much Hashem loves us. When we recognize the countless acts of kindness and concern that Hashem showers upon us, we can't help but feel happy.

But as with all middos, in order for our children to absorb hakaras hatov it must be modeled. Only by seeing us showing gratitude will they acquire this middah. Of course, we have just as much reason to show hakaras hatov as our children do. After all, who doesn't want to be happy?

Have you ever noticed
The way you start your day?
Did you ever pay attention
To the first words that you say?

"Modeh Ani" means "I give thanks"
To Hashem, the greatest King,
And throughout our day we try
To say thanks for everything!

Well, dear friends, listen well
And come along. You'll see
That you can be makir tov
And be as grateful as can be!

As Dovi finished his homework,
He felt his stomach groan.
"Oh, boy, do I feel hungry!"
He said with a slight moan.

When he walked into the kitchen,
Dovi's eyes opened wide.
His mother had made a tasty meal
And was serving it with pride.

Meatloaf and potatoes,
And a nice, big salad bowl,
Broccoli and mushrooms,
And yummy garlic rolls.

The table was all ready
For his family to dine.
Dovi took a deep breath ...
The smell was just divine.

"Mommy, I'm so grateful
That you took the time to shop,
And prepare and plan and cook,
And bake and set and chop!"

Dovi hugged his mother
And said "Thank you!" with a smile.
"Mommy, come sit down as well —
You've been working for a while!"

Of course, Dovi made a brachah
Before he began to eat.
"Thank you, Hashem, for all this food!
Each bite is such a treat!"

MEET DINA

Today was color war in camp.
What a smile on Dina's face!
She volunteered for her team,
To run the relay race.

But during the race she slipped
And she fell down with a thud!
"Ow!" she cried in pain,
Trying to wipe off all the mud.

Tears sprang from her eyes
And fell down to her chin.
She noticed she was bleeding
From cuts deep in her skin.

The camp nurse rushed over
And wiped her wound all clean.
She put on creams and band-aids
Until no more cuts were seen.

She spoke in such a soothing voice,
It made Dina feel so calm.
She even put a smiley stamp
On Dina's right-hand palm.

One week later, her cuts all healed,
Dina told the nurse:
"I made you something special
To keep inside your purse.

"I'm so grateful that you helped me,"
She had written on the card.
"You're the #1 camp nurse.
Thanks for working so hard!"

And then, "Thank you to Hashem," she said,
"For making my cuts heal.
My body works in wondrous ways —
It's a miracle so real!"

MEET BENNY

Benny's brother was a chosson!
Excitement filled the air!
The wedding would be out-of-town.
He'd get a brand-new suit to wear.

Benny counted down the days
Until the wedding date,
When he'd dance with all his cousins.
He could hardly wait!

Finally the day arrived,
And Benny waved good-bye
To all of his good friends
But then let out a sigh ...

"I'm sad I'm missing school,
Because our Rebbi is the best!
And I'm also a bit nervous
About our Chumash test.

"I'll have no time to study
During the time I'm away.
I should have planned ahead instead
Of just remembering today."

Rebbi overheard and smiled.
"Benny, have no fear ...
You just enjoy the wedding
While we're thinking of you here!

"When you get back to class,
I'll be glad to help you out!
I'll study with you for the test.
You'll do well, I have no doubt!"

When Benny came back to school,
Rebbi was all ready.
He helped Benny during his breaks,
And they studied slow and steady.

When they finished the review,
Benny did just fine!
Rebbi's help and caring
Really helped Benny shine!

Benny gave Rebbi a sefer
With a message that he wrote:
"I'm grateful to have such a Rebbi.
That's why I wrote this note!"

And then Benny thanked Hashem
For giving him a Rebbi who was great.
Rebbi's caring was something
He would always appreciate!

Bina woke up in the morning,
And her heart was filled with dread.
She was nervous to go to school
And wanted to stay in bed.

She looked down at the cast
That went from her ankle to her knee.
She had taken quite a fall
When she tried to climb that tree.

She stared down at her crutches —
Her only way to walk.
What would she do at recess ...
Just sit around and talk?

What about Machanayim ...
Would she miss out on the fun?
Would she have to sit alone,
Unable to play or run?

But Bina got ready anyway,
And her father gave her a ride.
Bravely, on her crutches,
She hopped her way inside.

When recess finally came,
She expected her friends to leave.
But instead they had a surprise for her ...
One she could hardly believe!

Her friends took out from their backpacks
Board games of every shape and size.
"We're staying inside to play with you!"
Tears of joy came to her eyes.

"Thank you, Hashem, for such special friends!"
Bina said with a big grin.
And to her friends, she said, "I'm so grateful!
Now let's play and see who'll win!"

Dovi, Dina, Benny, and Bina
Were each grateful to another.
They made sure to thank Hashem,
Their friend, teacher, nurse, and mother.

But the most important thing to know
Is what this means for you —
By saying "thank you" and being grateful,
You can be a makir tov, too!

PARENTS!
MAKE COPIES OF THESE "HAKARAS HATOV NOTES" TO GIVE YOUR KIDS WHEN THEY SHOW GRATITUDE!

I SAID THANK YOU TODAY!

I SHOWED MY APPRECIATION!

I GAVE MY PARENT A THANK YOU HUG!

I GAVE SOMEONE A THANK YOU NOTE!

MORE JUDAICA PRESS BOOKS

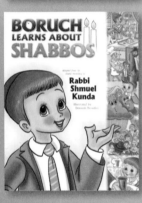

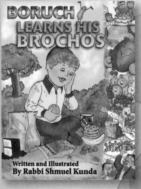